For Hannah and Ian —J.D.

For Liz, with love —A.C.

Henry Holt and Company, LLC
Publishers since 1866
175 Fifth Avenue
New York, New York 10010
www.henryholtchildrensbooks.com

Henry Holt® is a registered trademark of Henry Holt and Company, LLC.
Text copyright © 2004 by Julia Donaldson
Illustrations copyright © 2004 by Anna Currey
All rights reserved.
First published in the United States in 2006 by Henry Holt and Company
Originally published in the United Kingdom in 2004 by Macmillan Children's Books,
a division of Macmillan Publishers Limited, London

Library of Congress Cataloging-in-Publication Data
Donaldson, Julia.
One Ted falls out of bed / Julia Donaldson ; illustrated by Anna Currey.—1st American ed.
p.   cm.
Summary: When a teddy bear falls out of bed, he has an exciting playtime before finally managing to get back where he started.
ISBN-13: 978-0-8050-7787-2
ISBN-10: 0-8050-7787-1
[1. Teddy bears—Fiction. 2. Counting. 3. Stories in rhyme.] I. Currey, Anna, ill. II. Title.
PZ8.3.D7235One 2006   [E]—dc22   2005012173

First American Edition—2006
Printed in Belgium

1 3 5 7 9 10 8 6 4 2

One Ted Falls Out of Bed

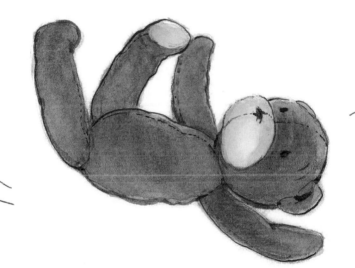

JULIA DONALDSON
ILLUSTRATED BY ANNA CURREY

Henry Holt and Company
New York

One ted
Falls out of bed.

He tugs and pulls the covers, BUT . . .

Two eyes are tight shut.

He jumps and shouts and makes a fuss,

Till three mice say, "Play with us!"

They roar around in four fast cars,

Then sit and gaze at five bright stars.

They sip some tea with six kind dolls

And have a fight with seven trolls.

They take a trip with eight balloons

To where nine frogs are playing tunes.

But one ted
Is missing bed.

Cheer up, Bear—
Build a stair.

One, two, three,   four, five, six,

Seven, eight, nine,
TEN RED BRICKS!

Ted is at the very top
When . . .

. . . ten bricks crash,
nine frogs hop,

And eight balloons go
BANG SNAP POP!

Seven trolls start running riot.
Six dolls whisper, "Shush! Be quiet!"
Five stars shine as bright as day.
Four cars toot and roar away.

Three mice scamper off to hide.

Two eyes open wide,

And one ted . . .

Is back in bed.

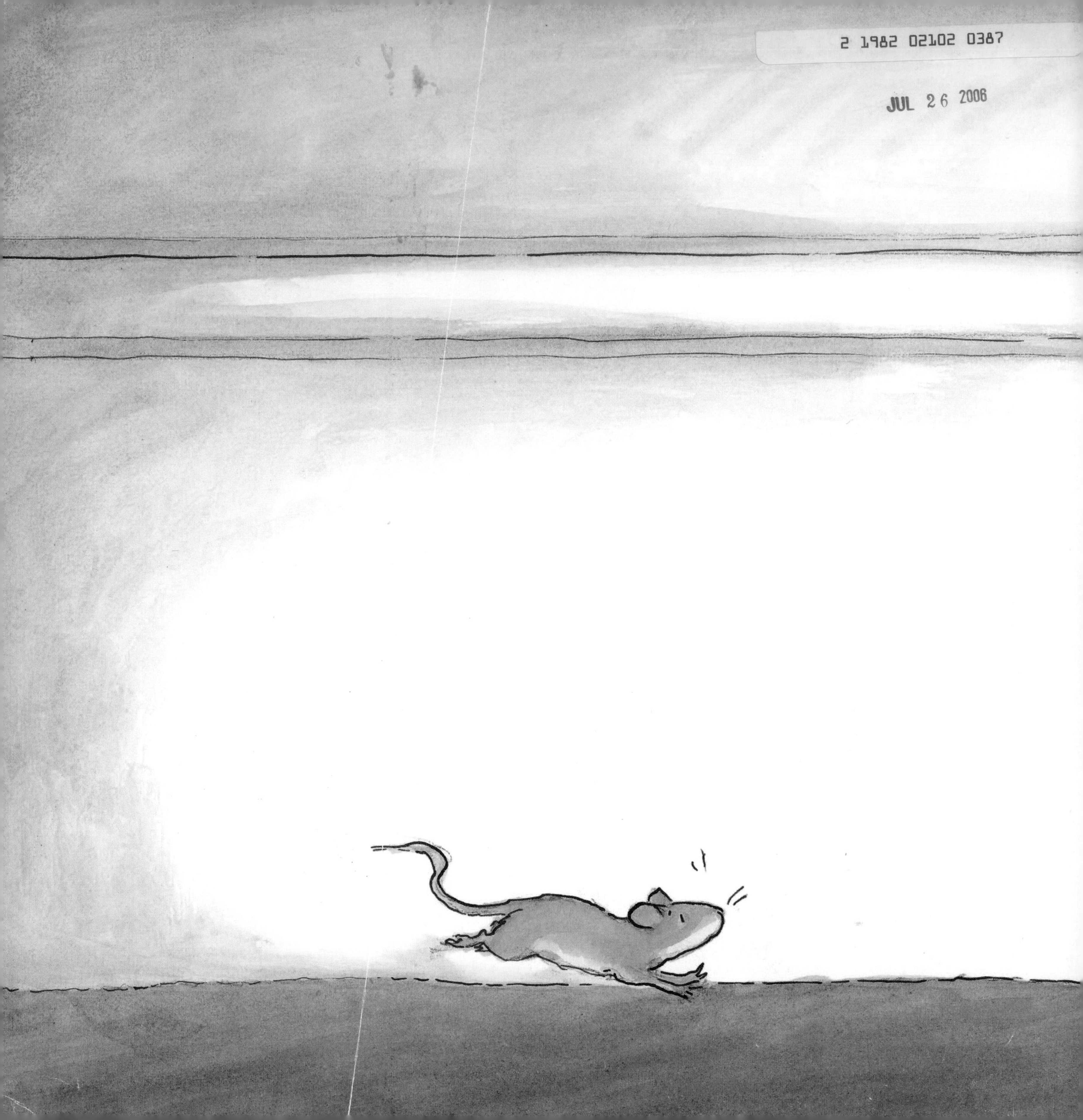